WORLDS COLLIDE
CRAFTERS' CLUB SPECIAL EDITION #1

AN UNOFFICIAL MINECRAFT NOVEL

LOUISE GUY

Copyright © Louise Guy 2017
First edition: 2017
Printed by Go Direct Publishing Pty Ltd.

Print ISBN: 978-0-6480144-4-7

Edited by Kat Betts

For the real-life JJ and Jamie.

CHAPTER ONE

A New Adventure

JJ stacked the last of the dishes in the dishwasher and switched it on. He grinned as his eye caught sight of a picture of himself, Jamie, and Sam on the fridge. He wondered what his cousin was doing. Probably trying to find his own real-life portal knowing Sam. JJ never thought he'd say it, but he missed having Sam around.

His parents came into the kitchen breaking into his thoughts.

"We're going to pop next door and get the Robinson's place ready," his mother said. "We'll only be about half an hour." She opened the fridge and took out a pile of containers.

JJ smiled, it was just like his mother to cook meals for their friends and welcome them home. Charli and her family had been away for the last ten days on a family vacation. JJ's parents had kept an eye on their house. His father had even cut their lawns that afternoon and trimmed the hedge out the front.

"Okay," JJ said. "I'll go and find Jamie. Do either of you know where he is?"

JJ's dad rolled his eyes and started humming. His tune perfectly mimicked the music from Minecraft.

JJ laughed. "I guess that means he's playing on the Xbox."

"Tell him he'll need to turn it off and get ready for bed as soon as we get back," his dad said.

"Will do." JJ left his parents organizing supplies and went in search of Jamie.

Minecraft music increased in volume as JJ approached the family room. He hadn't played much Minecraft since their last adventure. He'd been so busy with school and soccer training there was little time for anything else.

"Hey bro," Jamie said as JJ flopped down on the couch next to him. "Grab a controller and join if you want to."

"Nah, I think I'll just watch," JJ said.

Jamie's on-screen character, JamieG14, stopped moving as Jamie turned toward JJ. "Really? You've hardly played lately, are you sick of Minecraft?"

JJ shrugged. "Not sick of it, just taking a break."

Jamie nodded and returned his focus to the screen. "Charli's home tomorrow. We should go back through the portal. Don't forget, you promised

3

us the most awesome adventure yet when Sam left."

JJ sat in silence watching JamieG14 build a mountain of TNT. He had promised them an awesome adventure. He hadn't forgotten. He knew exactly what he wanted to do, but he wasn't sure whether it was possible. He would give the group the choice of which map they wanted to enter, as long as it had tall mountains, or an area where they could build a high platform.

Half an hour later the front door opened and his parents called out to them.

Jamie groaned as they were told to turn off the Xbox and get ready for bed. "It's Friday night, what difference does it make how late we play?"

JJ laughed and stood up. "My soccer match is at eight o'clock in the morning, so it does matter."

"Charli will be home by ten o'clock tomorrow," Jamie said. "While you're at soccer I'll organize for her and Annie to come over so we can make plans."

Nervous excitement pulsed through JJ as Jamie spoke. Each adventure into the Minecraft world had been amazing. Scary, thrilling, yet exciting. His idea for their next adventure shouldn't bring any trouble with it, but they'd thought that each time they'd entered the Minecraft world. So far they'd been proven wrong every single time.

Laughter drifted down the hallway from the family room as JJ pushed open the front door and entered the house. His soccer bag was slung over one shoulder and he could hardly contain his grin of excitement. His team had defeated the top team in the league by one goal, a goal he'd kicked in the final seconds of the match. His first goal for the season and his team's first win. It had been awesome. Hearing the laughs of his brother and two best friends coming from the family room stretched his grin even wider.

He deposited his dirty soccer kit in the laundry, grabbed a drink from the kitchen, and made his way to the family room.

"I think it will be a texture pack," Annie was saying.

Three excited faces turned as he entered the room.

"JJ!" Charli's smile was wide. "It feels like ages since I saw you."

JJ laughed and sat down on the couch next to Annie. "That's because it has been. How was your trip? You look really tanned."

"Fiji was amazing," Charli said. "We snorkeled and went on Jet Skis. Best holiday ever."

"But not as good as going into the Minecraft world," Jamie said.

Charli laughed. "No, but good in its own way.

"Sounds amazing," Annie said.

JJ nodded. "I've always wanted to be able to fly and this is a way it's possible."

"But if we're in survival we'd have to go the End City to get them, we can't do that without defeating the ender dragon," Jamie said.

"We're not doing that," Annie said. "No way. Not after what we learned when we visited the End. There's no way we hurt the dragon"

JJ shook his head. "I wasn't suggesting we do that. I hoped we might be able to go through in creative or, assuming we end up in survival, try and load elytra into chests before we go in. It's worked before."

Jamie shrugged. "But if it doesn't what sort of adventure is that? We go in and do nothing? Hardly sounds like the most awesome adventure yet."

JJ laughed. "Don't be so negative. Who says the chests won't work?"

"Let's at least give it a try," Annie said. "I'd love to be able to fly."

"Okay, let's create a new map." JJ picked up a controller. "We'll load in some chests and see what happens."

The four friends watched as a new map loaded on the Xbox. JJ quickly opened the inventory box and started choosing items to store in chests. The elytra was the first item.

"They look cool," Annie said.

"Put in spare elytra in case we damage one," Charli said.

"Great idea." JJ added extra elytra to the chests.

"Don't forget cakes and other supplies," Annie said. "There's no point being hungry."

The others laughed. JJ filled a chest with cakes, pork chops, baked potatoes, steak, bread, golden apples and watermelon.

"Weapons and healing potions would probably be more useful," Jamie said.

JJ nodded and filled a chest with weapons and potions, then added obsidian and flint and steel. "In case we have any portal problems," he said.

He finished filling the chests then stacked them neatly next to a lake. "Hopefully if we leave the map open here we'll all end up next to the chests when we go through the portal."

"Why don't we all join the map," Charli said. "If we put the elytra on now we might arrive in the map wearing it and not have to worry about chests and things."

Heat rushed to JJ's face. Why hadn't he thought of that? It was a much simpler solution. "Good idea."

The other three grabbed controllers. It only took a few minutes and JJLee45, JamieG14, CakeGirl1, and Charli9 were all wearing elytra wings.

"Check this out," Jamie said. He moved JamieG14 to the top of a mountain and ran off, his character immediately glided over the landscape below. "This would be so awesome to do for real," he said.

The others nodded in agreement, all their Minecraft characters were now using their elytra to glide.

"Let's build a wooden platform on top of the mountain," Charli said. "It will be easier to run off than just running on the grass. It might be rocky."

"You don't have to run with elytra," Jamie said. "We could just step off the mountain."

"It works better if you run," JJ said. "You might tumble down the mountain if you haven't got any speed."

Charli grinned. "And it would be much more spectacular to run or even sprint off the edge of a mountain."

"It would," Annie agreed.

JJ selected wooden blocks and started to build the platform. It was fifteen blocks long, five blocks wide and the end pointed off the side of the mountain and hovered over the valley below. Concern crossed his face and he looked up at the others. "If it doesn't work, we've got nowhere to go but down. It's a pretty big drop."

"It'll work," Jamie said. "If it doesn't we'll just crash to the ground and our health will be damaged. If the chests are full of food and healing potions we should be able to fix ourselves pretty quickly."

"Unless we die," Annie said.

Silence fell among the group.

"It is a possibility," JJ said. "Hopefully a slim one. We'll work out how to use the elytra before anyone runs off the platform. We'll make it as safe as possible."

Jamie grinned. "You must really want to fly, JJ. It's so unlike you to suggest something dangerous."

JJ shrugged. "We've ended up in so many threatening situations I hardly consider this dangerous. Like I said, we'll work out how to activate the elytra before we do anything that could end us in trouble. Now, everyone move to the top of the mountain and onto the platform and hopefully that'll be our arrival point when we go through the portal. We can go and find the chests later."

Soon all four characters stood on the mountain. Four remotes were deposited onto the coffee table and the Crafters' Club members rose to their feet.

"Time to visit the portal," JJ said.

The four friends traced the well-trampled path through the forest, across the now dry creek bed and up the other side. They moved into the clearing and stopped.

Charli grinned. "This still blows me away every time I see it."

JJ agreed. The large glowing portal was an amazing sight.

"It's surprising no one else has found it yet," Annie said.

"A few have," Jamie said. "Remember the professor?"

Annie shuddered. "Don't remind me."

The other three laughed. Annie was right, the professor was someone no one wanted to remember.

"Let's hope this adventure goes to plan," JJ said. "We'll step through the portal together, end up on top of the mountain wearing the elytra and spend some time gliding around. Then we'll come back through the portal and go home for some food."

"Sounds great," Annie said.

"Sounds highly unlikely." Charli pointed at the portal. "I don't think we've stepped through the portal once and things have gone to plan."

JJ smiled as he stepped toward the purple light. "Follow me," he said. "I've got a feeling that today's going to be different, today it will go to plan."

He stepped into the portal's flickering purple light with Jamie, Annie, and Charli close behind.

CHAPTER TWO

Elytra

Jamie's heart raced as he spun and twisted through the portal's bright lights eventually slowing as he arrived in the Minecraft map. He was excited. Their last trip through the portal had taken them to the End. The darkness and eerie noises they'd encountered were unnerving. He breathed with relief as his eyes adjusted to his surrounds. Trees, hills, lakes, and an endless blue sky rolled out before him. He was standing on top of the platform, exactly where he'd left his JamieG14 character when playing on the Xbox.

He looked down, checking he'd arrived in his Minecraft skin. His blue warrior costume gleamed in the sunlight but he felt heavier this time, weighed down.

Within seconds CakeGirl1, JJLee45, and Charli9 were standing by his side.

"See," JJ said, adjusting his red tie. "We arrived exactly where were wanted to."

"I'm wearing the elytra." The excitement in Annie's voice was obvious.

Annie was right, her pink-and-white cake-girl body now had the addition of gray wings.

"We all are," Charli said.

Jamie nodded. That explained why his back felt heavy. "I can't believe it worked, that we actually arrived in the right spot wearing elytra. It's unbelievable! Knowing our track record something has to go wrong."

"Nope, not this time," JJ said. "Look." He pointed to the base of the mountain.

Jamie peered over the edge of the platform and could just make out the square shapes of the four chests. He grinned. "So we've got everything we need. I wonder if we're actually in creative? Let's check our inventory and—"

Just as the words left Jamie's mouth a small explosion erupted causing the four friends to stumble.

"What was that?" Annie asked, righting herself. "A creeper?"

"No, it couldn't be," Jamie said. "You have to be almost next to a creeper before it explodes."

"Unless someone or something else is here," Charli said. She moved to the platform's edge and looked down. "I can't see anyone." She moved from each side of the platform to check further. "Whatever it was must have been blown up in the explosion."

19

"If it was a creeper we're most likely in survival," JJ said. He punched at his left arm and his inventory pad appeared. He quickly checked its contents. "It's not empty at least," he said. "I've got some food, plenty of iron and other blocks, and a few weapons." The others all checked their inventory and discovered they had items, too.

Annie grinned. "That's a nice change. When we add in the items from the chest we'll be really safe."

"Assuming whatever just exploded isn't going to be an issue," JJ said. "Let's plan to stay only during daytime, okay. Nighttime is when we lose a lot of health through attacks. We can always come back tomorrow and do it again."

The other three nodded. "Good idea," Annie said. "Even though I'm not as scared as I used to be, I'd still rather avoid mobs."

"Okay," Jamie said. "Enough talking, time to fly."

JJ peered over the mountain's edge. There were a few ledges and jagged sections of rock below but the platform was sticking so far out from the edge of the mountain that it was mainly empty space between them and the ground.

"How do you think it's going to work?" Annie asked. "Do we just run and jump off?"

"That's all you do out on the Xbox," JJ said.

"But you still need to press the A button to glide," Charli said. "What's the equivalent of the A button?"

The four Crafters' Club members stared at each other. They'd arrived with the right equipment but how were they going to use it?

"I guess we just try," Jamie said. "I think just run off the edge and see what happens."

The other three stared at him.

"Really?" Annie said. "That's your plan? JJ said we were going to work out how to use the elytra before we actually tried it."

Jamie laughed. "We learned to sprint by trial and error, this shouldn't be much different. My guess is I hold my left arm out as if I'm sprinting and it will have a similar result. I bet you I'll fly."

"Except you'll fall and crash if you don't get it right," Annie said. "You might hurt yourself."

Jamie rolled his JamieG14 eyes. "And I might just fly around. Move out of the way. I'll glide down toward the chests and we can check them out."

The other three moved as Jamie walked back to ensure he had a decent run up.

He thrust his left arm out in front of him and immediately sprinted along the platform to the edge of the cliff. Without hesitation, he stepped off and plummeted downward.

Annie's gasp echoed in the valley below as they watched Jamie hurtle headfirst toward the ground.

The ground below raced up to meet Jamie as he plunged toward it. Sprinting off the edge of the cliff had been easy but the elytra definitely weren't working. His heart raced as he tried to think of another solution. His left arm was still outstretched, maybe that was the problem. He pulled it close to his side. Nothing changed, he continued his free fall downward. He could see a large blue lake at the base of the mountain. If he were lucky it might break his fall. Only moments from impact, Jamie realized he wasn't going to be lucky. A large pit of lava sat between the base of the mountain and the lake and he was heading straight for it. He wasn't gliding, just falling fast. Hopefully he would die instantly and be thrown out of the map and back into the real world. The question was, would he be able to come back in again? A lump caught in his throat as he headed straight for the lava. At the last second he closed his eyes and stretched out both arms as if to shield the rest of himself from the impact.

Immediately he was swung onto his front and started to glide. He opened his eyes. The lava and lake were below him. Sweat poured down his face from the heat of the lava. He could almost reach down and touch it. Once over land, the tops of bushes bristled against his body as he glided above them. The sensation was amazing, with his arms outstretched he felt like Superman. He looked ahead and could see a hill poking up. He was flying straight at it. He needed to quickly work out how to move from left to right, how to go down and to stop. He moved his right arm so it pointed to the side, his arms now shaped like an L. He changed direction at once, turning to the right and continuing to turn until he moved his right arm back to its position straight out in front. He tried the same with his left and found himself turning to the left.

He'd worked out the turns. With his arms back in front of him he raised his head slightly and looked up. He immediately started flying upward. He raised his head again and flew higher. He knew he wouldn't go very high. Elytra only allowed you to go up momentarily. His heart raced as he waited to descend. He'd flown around the hill now and should try to land and make his way back to the others. He put his arms straight out above his head as he looked for a good place to land. But, rather than descending further, he was gliding straight up. He went higher and higher. Sweat beaded on his brow. This wasn't right, there must be a glitch. He half expected to go tumbling down to the ground at any second. He used his new-found controls to guide himself back to the mountain where JJ, Annie, and Charli stood watching. He approached the top of the mountain from above it and as he moved closer to his brother and friends pulled his arms down beside him. His body straightened into a standing position and he stopped.

He grinned as his feet touched the platform next to the others. Annie's mouth hung open in amazement.

"That was awesome," he said. "You have to try."

"You nearly died," Annie said. "We saw you heading straight for that lava. What happened?"

Jamie quickly explained how he'd found it difficult to work out how to control his movements. He told them what he'd discovered.

JJ's JJLee45 mouth turned down in a frown. "You flew upward, how was that possible?"

Jamie shrugged. "I have no idea. I looked up and went up a little bit but when I put my arms above my head and looked up I flew in that direction."

JJ shook his head. "But you can't do that with elytra. On the PC I held a firework rocket once and went really fast, but not much higher."

"I think we've found some kind of glitch," Jamie said. "There's no other good explanation."

"Not one that we know of," Charli said.

"A good glitch for a change," Annie said. "Let's hope there aren't any bad glitches in this map." She turned to Jamie. "So, two arms out straight to glide?"

Jamie nodded.

"And by your side to slow down and stop." Charli tried out the movements.

"Let's all get airborne and then we'll glide around and land by the chests," Jamie said. "We need to load the items into our inventory."

The other three nodded and one by one they lined up on the platform behind Jamie.

JJ was the last in line for takeoff. He watched as Jamie, Charli, and then Annie sprinted toward the mountain's edge. He'd been amazed to see Annie's CakeGirl1 character run straight off the edge of the platform. Like Jamie and Charli before her, she had glided straight away. All three were bunched together, waiting for him to join them.

JJ took a deep breath, thrust his left arm out in front and sprinted. He closed his eyes as he stepped out into thin air and put his right arm out to join his left. Immediately he was flying. He opened his eyes, overcome by the sensation of soaring through the air. He was actually doing it! They all were. JJ quickly tested his ability to turn left and right. He found that by reaching both hands out toward the ground he would fly downwards. He tilted his head up, as Jamie had instructed, and pushed his arms above his head. Immediately he flew up.

A huge grin spread across his face. Not only did the elytra work but a glitch meant they could really fly. He knew when he scored the goal at soccer that morning that it was going to be a good day. Now that he had his bearings he flew to the others. As he got closer he realized that it was going to be difficult to talk to each other while they were flying. Jamie must have realized the same thing and flew out in front of the group, indicating for them to follow.

JJ whooped with delight as he flew behind Jamie with the girls next to him. They swooped up and down, turned from left to right, flying over the most amazing scenery as they did. Lakes, mountains, villages, animals—they were seeing it all. Jamie approached a waterfall and flew down close to it. Sheep and chickens roamed around the base of the falls but there was nothing else to see. He flew back up and in the distance JJ saw a large mountain. They were so far from it he couldn't quite work out whether the white above it was cloud or smoke. He tried to catch up to Jamie to point it out but Jamie was gliding quickly and had already turned back toward their original starting place. They glided over more landscapes, past different types of trees and animals, and eventually came to a stop back at the base of the mountain.

JJ's face felt tight as his feet touched the ground and he stopped. The combination of grinning so much and the wind hitting his cheeks had left its mark. He could see from the bright cheeks of the others that they'd all experienced the same.

"That was awesome," Charli said. "Imagine if we

could fly like that at home! I'd never walk anywhere again."

JJ laughed. "It would be amazing, but it's still incredible we can do it here."

"Definitely," Jamie agreed.

"Look," Annie said. "We've landed right by the chests."

Jamie grinned. "Yep, figured we'd need to replenish our hunger by now. Let's get to those cakes and have a feast."

They each punched open a chest.

"Mine's empty," Charli said.

CakeGirl1's smile turned to a frown. "Mine too. I hope one of you boys has the chest with the cakes."

JJ opened his chest. "Empty."

"So's this one," Jamie said.

"Did anyone have spare elytra in their inventory?"

Charli opened her inventory pad. "We don't have the

spares JJ put in the chest and we're going to need new ones. Look at how badly worn these are already."

JJ looked at Charli's elytra wings. She was right. They would need to be replaced or repaired before they could fly again. He thought they would have lasted longer but then remembered that they had been flying around with the elytra on when playing from the Xbox. They must have taken some damage then, too.

"There's no spares," JJ said. "We should have tried enchanting them with mending before we arrived. We could make an anvil easily enough but getting an enchanted book isn't going to be easy."

"We'd need to find a librarian villager and trade for one," Jamie said.

"I think we might just have to give up on flying," JJ said. "It's a shame because I saw something in the distance I wanted to explore."

"What?" Jamie asked.

"It looked like a volcano," JJ said. "Although it might just have been a mountain with a large cloud on top."

"A volcano would be cool to fly over," Jamie said.

"Actually, it would be quite hot." The smirk on Charli's yellow face made the others groan.

"Let's go and check it out," Jamie said. "We should eat first and restore our hunger, then we will be ready to go."

"What about the damage to our elytra?" Annie asked. "Are we going to search for a villager?"

Jamie checked his inventory again. "No, we can fix them," he said. "They just won't be enchanted. I've got the tools to make an anvil and we also need leather."

"I've got a few pieces," JJ said.

"Me too," Charli added.

"Stand back then," Jamie said. "Time to get a crafting table, make an anvil and get ourselves back in the air."

❧

JJ and the girls watched as Jamie opened his inventory pad and placed a plank of wood into each of the four crafting squares. A crafting table appeared in the next box and he moved it down into his inventory. The dust on the ground beside them swirled slowly at first, then faster and faster. They closed their eyes as the dust churned. JJ grabbed onto Annie in order to steady them both as the wind blew them back and forth. Suddenly, everything stopped.

They opened their eyes. A nine-hole crafting table stood before them.

Jamie grinned. "Now to make an anvil." He opened his inventory again and selected four iron ingots and three blocks of iron. The items immediately floated before him. He moved the blocks of iron to the top three holes of the crafting table and one iron ingot into the middle square of the second row and the others to the bottom three squares. The wind immediately picked up, dust swirled, and the wind increased to a roar. The table lifted off the ground and spun faster and faster as the wind continued to lash against them.

JJ buried his head in his arms waiting for the elements to calm. Moments later they did and he was able to open his eyes. He grinned at Jamie. An anvil stood in front of them.

"Now we need to work out how to take our elytra off," Jamie said. "Then we add it to the first slot in the anvil and four pieces of leather to the second."

"Here," Charli said. She held her arms in the air and pointed to a lever under her left armpit. She pressed the lever and her elytra unclipped from her back and floated to the ground. The others did the same.

Jamie added his elytra to the anvil and JJ added all the leather from his inventory. They jumped back. They hadn't used an anvil before and had no idea how it would react.

Charli laughed as nothing happened. "We're all holding our breath wondering if it's going to explode or go crazy and it's doing nothing."

JJ and Jamie joined in her laughter.

"What an anticlimax," JJ said.

Annie tilted her head to one side. "No, listen," she said.

The others strained to listen. A soft yet high-pitched humming noise floated from the anvil. The noise grew louder until it was so intense that they needed to cover their ears.

The ground shook, at first a tremble, before breaking into huge wave-like movements. JJ stumbled as he was thrown sideways. As quickly as it had started, the high-pitched noise and shaking ground stopped. Smoke poured from the anvil and a small explosion occurred. The smoke cleared and Jamie's elytra appeared as good as new.

"Charli, can you add your leather to the anvil?" Jamie said. "JJ didn't have much and we might need some more. Then we just need to add everyone's elytra."

Charli added the leather and they completed the repairing process another three times, covering their ears and doing their best to stay upright as the anvil completed its job.

"Perfect," Jamie said as he handed back each elytra. "Now, let's restore our health and JJ can lead us to the mountain or volcano or whatever he saw."

They searched their inventory for food items and quickly restored their health. "I would have liked some of that cake, Annie," Charli said.

Annie grinned, wiping the frosting off her CakeGirl1 face. "Sorry, I only had one and I was hungry."

"Don't worry," Jamie said. "My dad promised he'd make us a cake. We can have it later. For now, just restore your health and let's go. The sun is still high in the sky but nighttime tends to creep up on us in here."

"As do the creepers." Annie laughed.

They finished their food and made their way back to the top of the mountain and the launch platform.

"You go first, JJ," Charli said. "We'll follow."

JJ nodded. "Okay. We'll go and explore what I saw and then we'll land somewhere and build a portal. By then it will be time to go home."

"Hopefully the portal will take us home," Annie said. "That isn't always a guarantee."

"It will be today. It's my lucky day, things are going to go right." He grinned, stretched out his left arm and sprinted toward the mountain's edge.

JJ flew in the same direction Jamie had earlier, hoping he would catch a glimpse of the large mountain soon. He wasn't sure if it was a volcano but he hoped it would be. He loved volcanoes. Everything about them was exciting. It would complete a perfect day for him. Not only had he kicked a winning goal in soccer but here he was in the Minecraft world, flying. Exploring a live volcano would absolutely top it off. He glanced back over his shoulder and grinned as he saw Jamie, Annie, and Charli lined up next to each other flying behind him.

He turned to his right and noticed the air temperature drop as they passed over the waterfall. Spray hit his face causing him to blink. As he moved away from the waterfall he saw the peak of the mountain in the distance. His excitement built as they traveled closer. It was definitely a volcano. Smoke rose from the crater and a long river of lava flowed down one side. JJ couldn't believe it. He'd created volcanoes in Minecraft many times but had never just come across one like this. This one was far more spectacular than any volcano he'd ever built.

The other three moved up beside him and he shouted into the wind, hoping they could hear. "Let's fly around it, see how close we can get."

The four friends flew in a line around the volcano. At times the heat from the lava was so hot they had to fly higher so as not to get burned. JJ noticed that Annie kept flying off from the group, as if she were searching for something, but just as quickly would return.

JJ couldn't believe he was able to do this. They flew up over the top of the crater. Below the smoke the orange glow of lava shone brightly. The heat rising from the crater was intense. JJ found himself flying higher and higher to move away from it. Annie and Charli followed but he looked down and saw Jamie flying quite low. He couldn't imagine how his brother could stand the heat.

He squinted, something about the way Jamie was flying didn't look quite right. He wasn't gliding smoothly like he had been, he was making jerky movements and seemed to be going lower and lower. If he went much lower he would be below the top of the crater and risk crashing into it.

JJ willed Jamie to fly higher. He flew back around, circling high above Jamie. He saw his brother spin over onto his back, his elytra wings now beneath him. JJ's heart pounded. Something had gone wrong. If Jamie didn't correct himself and fly upward within a matter of seconds then he would plummet into lava.

CHAPTER THREE

Unexpected Biome

Jamie tried to correct himself. Sweat poured down his face and off his body and it was hard to breathe. He'd flown too close to the lava in the crater. He thought he could withstand the heat, but he couldn't. His elytra didn't feel as heavy as it had previously and he worried that it was damaged or burned. His eyes closed momentarily before he jerked them open. He was weak. The effort to remain in the air was using every bit of his energy.

He thrust his arms upward, silently praying he would fly up and out of the crater, but nothing happened. His heart raced. There was nothing he could do, he was going to crash into the lava and die in the Minecraft world.

JJ saw Jamie's arms fly upward. He could see that his brother was trying to correct himself, trying to fly up out of the crater, but nothing was happening. He had no time to think through a plan. He pointed both of his arms down and flew into the smoke and heat of the volcano's crater. Sweat rushed down his face and into his eyes. The combination of smoke and sweat caused him to scrunch his face. He reached Jamie in a matter of seconds, flew just below him and then pushed his arms straight up. He shot upward, his arms connecting with Jamie's JamieG14 skin and pushed it out of the heat and smoke and up over the crater's rim. JJ could feel his own energy draining.

They needed to land as quickly as possible.

Annie and Charli flew to them immediately, the girls taking one of Jamie's arms each while JJ continued to hold the weight of his brother's body.

"Let's fly straight down to the ground," JJ yelled. "He's taken a lot of damage."

The three guided Jamie down to the base of the volcano. Lava rivers were flowing in all directions and it was hot but not unbearable.

They landed awkwardly, JJ and Jamie crashing to the ground.

Jamie groaned, his face was smeared with black ash, his elytra almost completely burned.

"Are you okay?" Annie asked.

Jamie shook his head slowly. "So weak."

Charli opened her inventory and took bread, steak, and pumpkin pies and threw them out in front of her. Both Jamie and JJ immediately ate. The girls joined them. Within minutes their health was restored and Jamie and JJ pulled themselves up to their feet.

"What happened?" JJ asked Jamie.

"I got too close to the heat. My elytra was damaged and I couldn't fly out of there." He grinned at JJ. "You saved my life, bro, thank you."

JJ shook his head. "I shouldn't have had to. Couldn't you feel how hot it was flying that low?"

"How was I to know heat would damage elytra? It doesn't when playing on the Xbox."

"It's more than damaged," Annie said. "It's melted."

"That's okay," JJ said. "After that close call I vote we go home. That's enough excitement for today."

His words were met with silence.

"What?" he said. "I think we should go." He looked at Annie. "Why are you shaking your head?"

"I saw something I really hoped we could explore.

Did anyone else notice the strange-looking forest further on from the volcano?" Annie asked.

"Is that what you were looking at?" JJ said. "I noticed you flying off at one stage."

Annie's CakeGirl1 eyes squinted in concentration. "It looked really strange, kind of out of place. I swear I could see large mushrooms and possibly the roof of a house. A really large house, perhaps a mansion."

"A mansion?" Jamie said. "Are you sure?"

Annie nodded. "I think so."

"It's pretty unlikely a mansion is going to spawn in an Xbox map. I think you might be imagining things," JJ said.

"There's one way to find out," Jamie said. "Let's fly over and have a look."

"We'll need to repair the elytra again," Annie said.

"Easy," Jamie grinned. "We already have the anvil and there's still some leather. Let's do it."

He took the anvil from his inventory and immediately the ground began to shake and the wind whipped up. By the time the anvil was standing in front of them Jamie already had his elytra off and was adding it and the leather. They closed their eyes again as a storm swirled around them. Just as quickly as it had started it stopped and Jamie's elytra appeared as good as new.

"You'd better do yours, too," Jamie said to JJ. "It's been burned."

JJ hesitated before taking his off. They really should be going home. Staying now could only lead to trouble. He opened his mouth, about to voice his concerns, when he looked at the excited faces of Jamie, Charli, and Annie. He closed it again. He wasn't going to be the one to ruin this adventure. Instead he glanced to the horizon. "A visit to the area Annie's seen needs to be quick," he said. "The sun's still high but I imagine it will start to sink soon. We did say this was going to be a daytime only adventure."

"Okay," Jamie said. "Annie can lead us to where she saw the forest and we can fly around and have a look. Then we'll find a clearing to land in, make a portal, and go home. How does that sound?"

Jamie, Annie, and Charli looked to JJ, waiting for his reply.

"Sounds good. Let me fix my elytra and we'll go."

They all closed their eyes briefly as the anvil did its job. JJ's elytra was repaired.

"Okay," Annie said as JJ clipped the elytra back on. "My turn to lead." She turned from the group and looked around. She pointed at a nearby hill. "I think that's high enough to launch from, what do you think?"

Jamie nodded. "We can just jump from the edge this time. There's really no need to build a platform.

Let's go up and look for a good spot to run off."

The group moved from the base of the volcano across the treed landscape to the hill. It didn't take long before they'd climbed to the top.

"It's perfect," Jamie said. "Just jump, Annie. We'll all follow you."

Annie took a deep breath, grinned at the group and moved to the edge of the hill. Without looking back she stepped off. She dipped down then quickly corrected herself and flew in a straight line. One by one, Jamie, Charli, and JJ followed her off the edge and into the air.

Jamie stayed close to Annie as she flew toward the forested area she'd seen. He hoped they would find something interesting. So far this adventure had been fun, but not as exciting as their others. Flying around had been different but he loved the Minecraft world when it threw something unexpected at them.

Annie flew down low as they approached a very thick forest. It covered a large area and looked quite out of place among the rest of the scenery. Jamie saw glimpses of red as they flew overhead. Annie was right, she had seen mushrooms. Toward the middle of the wooded area the roof of a huge mansion could be seen poking up above the trees. Jamie's heart began to race. The scenery unfolding in front of him was unfamiliar yet familiar at the same time. He'd only seen it once before and that was playing on the PC. Jamie shook his head. This didn't make sense at all, he needed to talk to the others.

He flew up in front of Annie and pointed down to the ground with both hands. He immediately flew down and the others followed. Within seconds they stood next to a giant mushroom, surrounded by trees.

Annie shivered. "Where are we? The air temperature is cooler here."

"I'm pretty sure we've entered a roofed forest biome," Jamie said. "And this area surrounds a woodland mansion." He pointed. "That's the building over there."

"A roofed forest biome?" JJ's forehead creased with confusion. "How's that possible from the Xbox?"

"It's been added to the Xbox version," Jamie said. 'It's really rare, though. I've only found one playing on the PC and that was getting a special map with coordinates from a cartographer villager."

JJ frowned. "It's strange it would appear in an Xbox generated map then. The elytra had a glitch, now this."

"I'd love to explore the mansion," Charli said. "Can we?"

JJ shook his head. "I'm not sure that's a good idea. The glitches are beginning to worry me. What if the portal has a glitch, too, and we can't get home? I think we should check that we can get home before we do anything else. We might need to use all our energy and resources for that."

"Boring!" Jamie said. "Come on, JJ. We've just discovered something new, we should at least look."

"Don't get me wrong," JJ said. "I would like to, I'm just worried that we'll use up all our health and hunger and then find the portal takes us somewhere other than home. We could be in trouble—"

A piercing scream rang through the air.

Annie jumped. "What was that?"

Another scream punctured the air from the direction of the mansion.

"Was it a mob?" Charli asked. "It didn't sound like any mob I've heard before."

The scream was followed by a voice laced with terror. "Help! Felix, help me."

"It's a person," JJ said.

Jamie's heart began to thud. A real person? The last real person they'd come across in the Minecraft world was the crazy professor who'd caused so many problems.

He pulled his diamond sword from his inventory and turned to the others. "Select the best weapon you've got and follow me."

JJ, Charli, and Annie followed Jamie's instruction. None of them questioned his action as the screams for help continued.

Jamie led the small group through the shade of the dark oak trees, past more giant mushrooms and continued on toward the mansion. Jamie was relieved to see that all of the Crafters' Club members were holding swords. He made his way around a giant brown mushroom, through more trees to a grassed area directly in front of the mansion. There was no time to waste. He thrust out his left hand and sprinted to the mansion's entrance only slowing as he reached the front door. Excitement pulsed through him as the fear-laced voice continued to call for help. He wondered how much the others knew about woodland mansions and the mobs that might be inside.

Jamie followed the cries of "Felix!" through the doorway and into the foyer of the mansion. He stopped and waited for the others to catch up. The cries for help had stopped and the mansion was eerily quiet.

"Where do we go?" Annie asked.

Jamie stared down the corridors and wondered

the same thing. They really needed to hear the cry for help again. He opened his inventory, relieved to find he had plenty of torches. It was dark in the mansion and they would need them. He motioned for the others to stay behind him as he followed the plush red carpet that led to many different rooms. He lit a torch as they turned off from the corridor and entered a room.

"A pumpkin room," Charli said. "Check it out."

The four stood looking at the unusual layout of the room. Two rows of pumpkins grew either side of a narrow water source.

Jamie placed another torch, his head swinging from side to side as his eyes explored every corner of the room. His heart raced. He hadn't spent much time in a woodland mansion on the PC but he knew enough to know he needed to be alert. He was surprised none of the others had mentioned mobs.

"Look out!"

Jamie's thoughts were interrupted by JJ's cry and he swung around just in time to see a strange-looking villager moving in their direction. Its gray head and black robe with the yellow stripe down the middle confirmed it was an evoker. It grunted as it swiped the iron axe it held toward them. Jamie stepped forward, his diamond sword outstretched. Four slashes later a grunt erupted from the evoker before it vanished, leaving an emerald in its place. Jamie collected the emerald and turned to the others. He grinned. "One down."

"What was that?" Annie asked. "It looked like a type of villager."

"An evoker," JJ said. "There are different mobs in a woodland mansion. Evokers and vindicators are what we need to be on the lookout for."

"And vex," Jamie added. "Although if we quickly

57

kill any evokers we see they shouldn't be an issue. We're better to attack the evokers with a bow, if anyone has one? We want to limit the damage they can do to us."

They searched their inventories and discovered Annie was the only one with a bow.

Jamie grinned. "Next evoker is all yours, Annie."

Annie took the bow from her inventory and returned Jamie's grin. "Bring it on!"

JJ shook his head. He wasn't sure if he'd ever get used to Annie being so confident. She'd become daring, looking for adventure now rather than shying away from it. Deep down JJ knew they should really be leaving the mansion and ensuring they could return home safely, but Annie's adventurous side was contagious. Excitement pulsed through him. They'd

just been attacked by a mob most o
even seen when playing Minecraft o:
alone when they were in a map. He
they'd get a chance to see more.

JJ took his position behind Charli as Annie and
Jamie moved from the pumpkin room back into
the mansion's corridor. Jamie placed torches as they
followed the red walkway.

"Check out this room," Annie called. "It's
full of flowers." They poked their heads into the
room to discover five flowerpots boasting colorful
arrangements of red, orange, pink, and white flowers.

"It smells delicious in here," Charli said.

A scream swiftly brought them back to the task
at hand.

"It's coming from upstairs," Jamie said. "Come
on, let's hurry."

The four Crafters' Club members raced along the

dor and up a staircase to the second floor. They reached a landing. The grunting sounds of an evoker erupted from an open doorway.

Annie turned and aimed an arrow directly at it as it hurried toward the group, axe swinging wildly at them. Her arrow hit dead center and she reloaded and fired another and another. Within seconds the evoker disappeared leaving behind an emerald and its iron axe.

"Great job," Jamie said. "Grab the axe, Annie, that could come in handy."

Annie picked up the emerald and the axe as the cry of "Felix!" erupted once more.

"It's still above us," JJ said. "There must be a third floor."

Annie took the lead, her bow leveled as they bounded up the stairs to the third level. She stopped at the top of the stairs and another cry floated down the corridor. She pointed. "Whoever it is is down there. Get your weapons ready."

The four walked carefully in the direction of the cries, bow and swords out ready. They passed rooms shrouded in darkness as they moved toward the voice.

JJ could hear his own heart beating. The fear in the person's voice was obvious. He only hoped that this wasn't some kind of trap they were being led into.

The cries for Felix were drowned out by strange screeches and frightening screams as the four friends made their way slowly along the corridor.

"What is that?" Charli asked.

Jamie grinned. "Sounds like we might have found a vindicator."

"Why do you look so happy about it?" Charli's yellow forehead creased in a frown.

Jamie shrugged. "Because we get to meet another mob and hopefully defeat it. Come on, don't be a chicken, we've all got weapons, we'll be fine."

"He's right," Annie said. "Let's do it."

Charli's yellow head shook with disbelief. "Who are you?"

Annie laughed. "CakeGirl1 is a lot braver these days than real-life Annie."

"Whatever those mobs are," JJ said, "they're getting closer."

The noises had grown in volume.

"Let's find this person in trouble," Jamie said. He lifted his head and shouted. "We're here to help. Where are you?"

"Felix?" The voice traveled from a room further along the corridor.

Jamie took the lead, moving with caution as the screeches, groans and grunts intensified.

He looked into one room, quickly moving past as he saw three evokers roaming around it. He crossed the corridor and stopped at the doorway of a large dining hall. A number of tables were strewn throughout the room. A large chandelier hung from the center of the ceiling but that was not what caught Jamie's eye. He stopped and stared. In the middle of the room, surrounded by two vindicators and an evoker, stood a black-and-white panda. The gamer tag Pandy11 hung above its head.

There was no time to talk to the panda, the mobs immediately advanced toward the group, their axes swinging and their moans deepening. Annie shot arrows at one of the vindicators quickly killing it while Jamie took on the evoker, leaving the final vindicator to JJ and Charli.

Before Jamie had the chance to attack the evoker it raised its arms in the air and an off-white smoke poured from it. Its deep groans changed to a high-pitched horn-like sound.

"Look out," Jamie yelled. "It's spawning."

All attention turned to the evoker as it disappeared in the cloud of smoke. Three small winged creatures with large fangs took its place and immediately began to attack.

"What are they?" Charli yelled as she fended one off with her iron sword.

"Vex." Jamie brought his diamond sword down onto one. His sword was getting heavy to lift, he knew he'd been hit enough times that his health was declining. They needed to win this battle and quickly.

He breathed a sigh of relief as the vex was quickly killed by Annie and her arrows. The other two vex had been taken care of by JJ and Charli.

"The evoker's still alive," JJ said. "Annie, can you shoot it with your bow?"

Annie took aim at the evoker which had moved to a corner of the room as the vex attack took place. Purple smoke now erupted from it.

"What's it doing?" Charli asked.

"Hurry," Jamie called to Annie. "It's trying to launch a fang attack."

"Fang attack?" JJ said. "What's that?"

Jamie didn't get a chance to explain. Within seconds a line of sixteen blocks rose up from the ground, large snapping fangs attached to each one. They snapped at the air and disappeared again.

"They're gone" Charli called. "Come on Annie, get that evoker."

Before Jamie could warn her, Annie stepped toward the evoker, an arrow strung in her bow ready to shoot it. She pulled it back and released at the exact moment the fangs rose up from the floor. She was practically standing on top of them. She had no chance to move before the snapping jaws of one of the fangs gripped her leg and bit down hard.

CHAPTER FOUR

A Foreign Visitor

Fear pulsed through Jamie as Annie cried out. The fangs chomped down on her leg then disappeared into the floor again. The bow and arrows crashed to the ground as Annie's CakeGirl1 body crumpled in a heap.

JJ rushed to her. They needed to move her before the fangs reappeared. She wasn't moving. With Charli's help he pulled her to safety.

Loud grunts erupted from the corner of the room. The evoker looked like it was planning its next attack. Jamie picked up Annie's bow and launched an arrow just as the fangs snapped back up from the floor. This time no one was hurt, except the evoker. Jamie's shot was a perfect hit. He fired another and the evoker let out one final grunt before it vanished.

JJ shook Annie gently. "Annie, wake up. You're safe again."

Annie didn't respond.

"She's hurt," Charli said. "She was already weak but the attack has damaged her."

"Has anyone got a potion of healing?" JJ said.

They all checked their inventories, no one had.

Jamie thought for a moment, they needed to help Annie, and quickly.

"I can help."

The gentle voice came from the other side of the large dining hall. It was the panda. It moved toward them, punching at its arm as it did. An inventory pad, exactly the same as the one the Crafters' Club members could access, appeared. "I have a splash potion of healing."

The panda took the potion from its inventory and passed it across to where Jamie stood. "Please use it. You've just saved me, we need to save your friend."

Jamie nodded and took the potion. He took the lid off the red bottle and carefully splashed Annie with it. Nothing happened. Work, he willed it. He splashed a little more on her. Gradually she opened her eyes and smiled at three worried faces.

"Sorry, did I go to sleep or something?"

Jamie shook his head. "The fang attack, don't you remember?"

Annie frowned. "No, I remember being about to shoot an arrow at the evoker, did I get it?"

Jamie smiled. The potion had wiped Annie's memory of the event. It was probably a good thing as he guessed those fangs hurt.

"The evoker, he has been killed."

Annie and the rest of the Crafters' Club members turned to face the panda who had just spoken. Its voice was different, like he had an accent of some kind.

"Thank you for your help," JJ said. "That potion saved Annie's life."

A smile spread across the furry black-and-white face. "Then we are even as you have saved mine."

"Are you a real person?" Jamie asked. "Or do you live here and always look like a panda?"

Pandy11 shook his head. "No, I come from a different place to this. I am a human not a panda. I have entered here through a portal. Is that how you arrived?"

This time Annie answered. "Yes, we came through a portal. We've not met many other real people in a map."

"I've never met anyone," the panda said. "Except for Felix."

"Who's Felix?" Annie asked.

"My brother," Pandy11 said. "We came into the Minecraft world together but it was a different map. We got separated and I went back through the portal to go home but I ended up here instead. Felix is either back in the first map or he's made it home. I was trapped in the mansion by the evoker and vindicators before I could work out how to get back."

Jamie grinned. "You're just like me and my brother," he said. "Two bros who love Minecraft."

Pandy11 laughed. "Kind of."

"I'm Annie," Annie said. "CakeGirl1 is my gamer tag but call me Annie. And these guys are Jamie, Charli, and JJ. What's your name?"

"Max," Pandy11 answered.

"So, Max," JJ said. "You might be able to come

out through our portal and find your way home from there. I'm not sure how many real-world portals there are. You might find it is the same portal as the one you've been using."

"You're not Max Black, are you?" Jamie asked, thinking it could be the Max from JJ's year level at school.

Max shook his head. "No, Max Santos."

The sinking sun caught JJ's attention through one of the dining-hall windows. "It's going to be nighttime soon and our health and hunger are low. Why don't we go back out to the real world? Hopefully Max will find it's the same portal that he normally uses. If it is then he can find his way home, if it's not we'll have to think of another plan."

"We'll have to come back in if that happens," Jamie said.

"Maybe," JJ said. "Although Dad can probably

give Max a lift home if he doesn't live too far away."

He turned to face the panda. "What do you say, Max? Do you want to come out with us? Give it a go?"

Pandy11 nodded. "Thank you."

Jamie laughed. "Don't thank us yet, our portal will probably take us to the Nether or somewhere horrible. We're used to things not going quite to plan."

"I hope not," Max said. "Felix and I ended up in the Nether one time and it was scary and so hot. I said I'd never go there again."

"Don't worry," JJ said. "We're having a lucky day, we won't end up anywhere scary. Let's get out of the mansion and go and build a portal."

Jamie, Charli, Annie, and Max followed JJ out of the dining hall and back down the stairs to the second and then first level of the mansion. They encountered one more evoker along the way which Annie quickly disposed of.

"You're very brave with your bow," Max said.

Annie grinned. "It's becoming my favorite weapon."

They followed JJ out through the foyer and onto the grass at the front of the mansion. The sun was still hovering just above the horizon. They needed to be quick.

"I'm not going to build the portal here," JJ said. "This woodland mansion still feels like some kind of glitch with the map. I'd hate to imagine where we might end up if we leave from here. We'll go back out to the area that we know was built in the Xbox map."

"Hate to imagine?" Jamie said. "I'd love to know. It could be really exciting."

JJ shook his head. "Our job right now is to get

ourselves home and help Max, nothing else, okay?"

Jamie grinned. "Okay. We'll follow you, boss."

A short time later the five reached the edge of the forest and stepped back into the map generated by the Xbox. JJ motioned for the group to stop and opened his inventory.

Pandy11 and the others looked on as JJ threw the obsidian from his inventory and quickly built the frame of the portal. A whoosh went up as he used his flint and steel to light it.

"You're quick," Pandy11 said. "Very quick."

"Come on," JJ said. "Let's get you back to the real world and find Felix." He indicated for the others to line up next to him. "When I say three, everyone needs to step into the portal."

On his count of three, with Pandy11 by their side, they stepped into the portal and out of the Minecraft map.

JJ opened his eyes as he stumbled out of the portal, relief spreading through him immediately. It *was* their lucky day. His feet had landed on the soft grass of the clearing in the forest behind his house. Now all they needed to do was help Max find his way home.

JJ waited as first Annie, then Jamie, then Charli appeared. They grinned as they saw they'd arrived back safely. They all turned and watched the portal waiting for Max.

"You don't think he's ended up in a different map or in the Nether, do you?" Annie said.

JJ bit his lip and didn't respond. Come on, Max.

His frown turned into a smile as a foot, then a body pushed its away out of the portal and fell in a heap on the ground, followed by a large groan. A mop of black hair completely hid Max's face. This was so strange, meeting Max when he looked like a panda and now getting to meet the real boy. JJ imagined seeing all of them would be strange for Max, too.

Max pushed the hair from his eyes and turned to face the Crafters' Club.

JJ sucked in a breath and Charli let out a laugh. "Sorry," she said covering her mouth with her hand. "I think we all assumed you were a boy. The name Max and all."

Max frowned, her eyes searching their faces. "I didn't correct you, either. My real name is Maxima, but I hate it. I like to be called Max."

"Maxima is an unusual name," Annie said.

Max raised an eyebrow. "Really? There are a lot of girls called Maxima at my school. It is a very popular name, that's partly why I don't like it. I don't want to be the same as everyone else." She looked at each of the Crafters' Club members again. "You all look and sound very different to my family and friends. Are you on vacation?"

Concern was etched on JJ's forehead. Are we on vacation? The same could be asked of Max. The vibes he'd felt all day about this being his lucky day were rapidly disappearing. Max's question, appearance, and name suggested she might not be from around here.

"Is this the portal you use?" JJ asked.

Max shook her head. "No, our portal is very different. Well, the portal is similar but the surrounding area is different. We don't have so many trees, they have all been cleared. It is mainly rice fields. The portal is in an old area which was once flooded and is no longer used for farming, no one goes there anymore, except for Felix and me."

"I'm not sure where the rice fields are," Jamie said. "But our Dad will know. I'm sure he'll be able to take you home. You know your address, don't you?"

Max nodded. "I'm sure it is not around here though. I've never seen trees like these."

"Dad will be able to help," Jamie said. "He can solve any problem, can't he, JJ?"

JJ was staring at Max, his concerns growing by the second.

"JJ?" Jamie repeated.

"Sorry," JJ said. "I'm just a bit worried. We don't exactly have rice fields where we live, or even in our country." He turned to Max. "Max, what country do you live in?"

"The Philippines," Max said.

Annie gasped. "How's that possible?"

Jamie grinned. "Awesome! My dad definitely can't drive you home though."

"I can't believe you've traveled to a different country," JJ said. "I didn't realize it was possible."

"Neither did I." Max's eyes were wide, she looked scared. "I need to work out how to get home. I'll be in trouble if I'm missing for too long."

"Don't worry," Jamie said. "We'll get you home, won't we, JJ?"

JJ stared at Jamie. How on earth did he expect that to happen? But for Max's benefit he nodded and forced a smile. "Of course."

"You speak very good English," Charli said. "Do you speak another language, too?"

Max nodded. "Filipino and English. English is taught in our schools and my English is nearly as good as my Filipino."

"We should all come to the Philippines with you," Jamie said. "We'll have to go back in, find the portal you came through and take you back. I've never been to another country."

"No," JJ said. "Our only job now is to get Max

home. We're not going sightseeing or doing anything else. It'd be just our luck that something would go wrong and we couldn't get home. Okay?"

Jamie scowled, then nodded. "I guess so."

JJ stared at his brother. He knew Jamie well enough to know that he'd have to watch him, to make sure he didn't go off and get lost in another country. It was bad enough getting lost in the Minecraft world but so far they'd always managed to return safely. He couldn't begin to imagine trying to explain to his parents that Jamie was lost in Southeast Asia.

"We can go back now?" Max asked.

JJ nodded. "Yes, so much for my perfect, problem-free day. But I'm not sure we all need to go." He turned to the other Crafters' Club members. "Does anyone want to go back to my place and watch from the Xbox, be available if we need any help?"

Annie answered for all three of them. "No, we all

want to go back in, but shouldn't we try the Xbox first? See if we can explore the map quickly and find the portal Max came in from?"

"Good idea," JJ said. He turned to Max. "Come on, hopefully we can work out exactly where you got lost."

Max nodded then fell into step behind JJ, Jamie, Charli, and Annie as they walked away from the portal and into the thick forest.

∽

A few minutes later the five were sitting in JJ's family room, Xbox controllers in hand. Max seemed fascinated by everything, from the forest to JJ and Jamie's backyard, and now their house.

"This is very different to where I live," she said.

"Look," Annie pointed to the screen. "The map's showing the exact point we left from. There's the portal and the volcano is in the distance."

"Did you realize you're on Xbox Live?" Charli turned from the screen to face Jamie.

"So?" Jamie said. "What difference does it make?"

"I'm just wondering if that's how Max ended up in our map. Were you using Xbox Live?"

Max nodded. "Felix was. He wanted to see if it made any difference, if we'd meet anyone else in the map. I was playing on my PC at the time. I'd just found the woodland mansion and wanted to explore it, I never thought it would appear in the map though. We've only seen maps we've created on the Xbox before."

"So have we, up until now," JJ said. "But the fact Felix was trying to meet someone in the map meant he thought it was possible."

Max nodded. "Except he didn't see anyone, only I did. He'll be really mad."

"Maybe you could bring him back next time," Jamie said. "Or we could meet you both in another map. If we find each other through Xbox Live and have the same map open before we go through our portals it might be possible."

Max nodded. "Felix would love that. He will be very envious that he did not get to meet you."

"Let's explore," JJ said, bringing their attention back to the task at hand. "See if we can work out how Max ended up in this map."

All five concentrated on the screen as JJ put new elytra on and glided around the map. "This is definitely a quick way to get around," he said. Ten minutes passed and other than the scenery changing from time to time, villages appearing on occasion and seeing different animals on the landscape, there was no sign of another portal.

"I arrived next to a lake," Max said. "There was

a village nearby and a lot of creepers. They blew up and destroyed the portal I arrived through."

"I think we need to find and repair the first portal you came through," JJ said. "It would most likely take you back to where you came from."

"We just need to find it," Charli said.

They watched as JJ continued to explore the map.

"Go back to the portal where we left the map," Jamie suggested. "It can't be too far from that spot. Just go in the opposite direction from last time."

JJ returned to the portal and this time took off in the opposite direction.

"Stop." Max pointed at the screen. "That looks like the village."

JJ slowed and brought JJLee45 down to the ground and began walking. Cows and chickens roamed the roads surrounding the village. A villager tended a vegetable garden.

"Go that way." Max pointed to the left of the screen. JJ followed her instruction and moments later found himself beside a lake. Blocks of obsidian were strewn around the area.

"That's the portal," Max said. "It really blew up."

"Shall we fix it?" Annie asked.

JJ hesitated. "I'm not sure it's worth fixing. I think it might be better to let Max fix it when we get back in. If it's her inventory it'll have the best chance of working how she needs it to. Fixing it from out here might mess it up in some way."

"We should all go back in," Jamie said.

JJ nodded. "Yes, let's leave the map exactly where it is now. Hopefully we'll end up near the village and portal when we return."

"The sun looks like it's sinking," Annie said. "Should we watch nighttime from out here and go back in once it is daytime again?"

JJ considered Annie's suggestion. "I'm not sure if that's necessary. We usually end up in the world at the start of daytime. I almost think it resets itself as we arrive. But, if it doesn't, by the time we walk back down to the portal now and go through it will probably be daytime again anyway."

"JJ's right," Jamie said. "It'll be daytime, of course we'll be fine."

Max grinned. "And if it's not then we can have some fun."

"Great," Annie muttered. "Endermen, zombies, creepers, spiders—definitely not my idea of fun."

JJ laughed as he stood and directed everyone out of the family room. "Come on, time for some international Minecraft travel."

The Crafters' Club members and Max retraced their steps through the forest, across the creek bed, and up into the clearing.

JJ turned to them as they neared the portal. "Ready?"

The others nodded and as a group they followed JJ's lead, stepping through the portal and back to the Minecraft world.

CHAPTER FIVE

Portal Hunting

JJ's eyes took a few moments to focus in the darkness as they arrived back in the map. Annie's groan was drowned out by Jamie's laughter.

"So much for always arriving in the daytime," Annie said. "Shall we go back out and come back a bit later?"

"No way!" Max and Jamie spoke at the same time. Jamie grinned at their new friend, now transformed into her Pandy11 skin. "This is an adventure," he said. "Between the five of us we should be able to fight off any mobs."

"At least we arrived where we hoped to," Charli said. "I can just see the outline of the village over there," she pointed, "and the glow of the volcano that way."

"That's the volcano Felix built," Max said. "He spent ages on the Xbox creating it, hoping it would be in the map when we arrived."

"That explains how it got here," JJ said. "I didn't think they just spawned in maps. It's amazing. Now," he turned his attention to their surrounds, "we need to work out how to get you home."

"Finding the damaged portal should be easy," Jamie said. "It was beside a lake right next to the village. Hopefully we'll have torches."

"Check your inventory," JJ said. He opened his inventory and looked up at the others. "Check what you've got. I've got a few weapons and a small amount of food."

Jamie, Annie, and Charli had similar inventories.

"How about you, Max?" JJ looked across to Pandy11.

Pandy11 shook her head. "Not much. Obsidian, flint and steel and a diamond sword, nothing else. At least I can repair the portal—" Max stopped talking, her furry black-and-white ears standing upright.

JJ strained to listen. What had Max heard? His heart thumped as he recognized a familiar sound. He turned to look at Annie.

"Enderman?" There was a slight tremble in Annie's voice.

JJ nodded. "You okay?" He watched as CakeGirl1's frown turned to a small smile. Annie took her diamond sword from her inventory and held it in the direction of the black creatures.

"Okay? I'm fine. Bring 'em on."

Jamie grinned hearing Annie's words. He called

to her as he launched an attack on the nearest mob. "This is no worse than the enderman attack when we were in the End. We'll destroy them easily."

The five were suddenly surrounded by the black creatures. There were at least twenty of them. A crunch-crunch sound, as if a wild creature was chomping on bones, filled the air. The sound was quickly drowned out by screams as the endermen spied them and launched an attack.

Screeches and hisses erupted as swords connected with the endermen. Each of the five were busy in their own battles, defeating one black creature then moving to the next.

JJ looked across to see Pandy11 taking on two of the mobs at once. She was quick on her feet, moving and darting out of the endermen's way, connecting with her sword at every opportunity. He was impressed. She had killed the two and was collecting their enderpearls in the same time he'd only killed one. Annie appeared just as skilled and in no time only an enderpearl hung in the air where the last enderman had been.

"Thank goodness." Annie's eyes focused on the horizon and rising sun. Nighttime lifted and the trees, hills, and grass came into view once more. "That's enough mobs and surprises for today. Let's get the portal repaired and get Max home. I'm ready to—"

An explosion shook the ground and filled the air with dust.

Annie's scream was drowned out when a second huge explosion erupted not far from where they stood.

"Take cover!" JJ yelled. He pushed Max behind a large group of rocks. Jamie, Annie, and Charli were quick to follow. They crouched low as smoke and dust filled the air and a third explosion detonated.

JJ couldn't work out what was happening. The explosions were too large to be creepers or any other type of mob they'd encountered before. The ground continued to rumble from the explosions. Huge holes had been blown in the landscape, the trees destroyed.

"Are we being attacked?" Annie asked.

JJ thought hard. It was the most likely explanation, but by who?

"No," Max said. "I think I know what is happening."

The four Crafters' Club members turned to the black-and-white panda waiting for an explanation.

"Felix and I have a backup plan for when we enter the Minecraft world. If we get lost or one of us doesn't come home then we blow up the map, hoping it will cause us to be taken back into the real world. Felix must be really worried to have acted on the plan."

"But if you die in the Minecraft world you won't be able to ever go back in," Jamie said.

"Are you sure?" Max said.

"Yes," Charli said. "We had two friends, the Wilson brothers, who died in a map. They were thrown out into the real world but they couldn't get back in through the portal. It's something we've been afraid could happen to us."

The ground shook again as a fourth explosion rocked the landscape.

"We need to get out of here," Jamie said. "If Felix is planning to blow up the entire map then we'll die."

JJ stepped out from behind the rocks. The landscape in front of him looked completely different from how it had moments earlier. Gone were the hills and trees. Gone was the lush green grass. In front of them, among the smoke, were huge crater-like holes where the TNT had exploded.

The other four moved out next to JJ. "If Felix is playing from the Xbox he should be able to see us in the map," Annie said. "Surely he wouldn't blow us up then?"

JJ glanced to his left. A trail of redstone dust ran alongside the rocks they had just been sheltering beside. "Run!" There was no time to answer Annie's question or explain. He pushed out his left arm and sprinted.

Annie, Charli, Jamie, and Max immediately followed. They were only a short distance from the rock pile when a deafening explosion threw them from their feet and flung them into one of the craters. Rocks and dirt sprayed against them when they landed.

JJ found himself face down on the ground. Loose debris continued to batter against his JJLee45 skin. He groaned and pulled himself up. He glanced around. Jamie, Annie, and Charli seemed to be piled one on top of each other while Max lay off to one side. A lump rose in his throat as he realized none of the others were moving. He quickly went across to help. He was relieved as he neared them to hear murmurs break out from the pile of bodies.

"Get off me, would you?" Jamie's voice was muffled, he was buried on the bottom of the pile.

JJ helped Charli and Annie to their feet. Part of him wanted to laugh at the look of horror on Jamie's face. It appeared he didn't like being squashed by the girls.

Max pulled herself to her feet and moved back to join the others.

"So much for seeing us and stopping his explosions," Annie said.

"I don't understand," Max said. "If Felix could see us he wouldn't hurt us. I'm worried he can't see us and if that is the case he will keep blowing up the map."

"He should be able to see us," JJ said. "We should be able to see his Minecraft character, too. Unless it's another glitch? We've had a few of those this time around." The Minecraft world was behaving differently. It was completely unpredictable which made it very dangerous.

"What are we going to do?" Charli asked. "Go back through the portal and take Max with us?"

JJ stared at Max. If they took her out with them they'd have to explain to their parents where she came from and that they'd met in the Minecraft world. None of them wanted to deal with the consequences of that. They'd never be allowed back in and Max would be traveling home on an airplane, not through a portal.

Slowly he shook his head. "Taking Max back

out with us would be the equivalent of dying in the Minecraft world. We'd never be allowed back in."

Jamie grinned. "So we might as well just solve the problem, or die doing it."

JJ glanced at the worried faces of Charli, Annie, and Max, and nodded. "There's no other option."

∽

Explosions continued in the distance as the five friends ate to restore their health then moved across the landscape in search of the portal. It wasn't easy walking with so much of the ground blown away.

"At least Felix has moved away from us," Annie said, steadying herself as the ground shook from an explosion in the distance.

"I can't believe he laid enough TNT to blow up most of a map," Jamie said. His eyes glinted with excitement. "I can't wait to meet this guy."

Another explosion caused the five to stumble. Jamie crashed into Charli sending her flying to the ground. He steadied himself before putting out a hand to help her up.

Charli looked around. "We can tell where we are by working out where the volcano is," she said. "At least he hasn't blown it up."

"Yet," Max said. "He's planted tons of TNT around it and redstone trails with repeaters leading from different parts of the map to it. There's enough to blow up a huge section of the map. He said it would be the last thing he blows up as he's pretty sure it would be devastating."

"Then we need to be quick," Jamie said.

The five friends retraced their steps across the broken landscape, back past the village to the lake where the pieces of the damaged portal lay.

JJ stopped, his eyes squinting at what looked like a

red rope lying along the road that led into the village. His heart thumped. It wasn't a rope. It was a very long trail of redstone dust. He could see redstone repeaters at various points along the trail. It went through the village and continued further, in the direction of the volcano. Felix must have set it up to work like a fuse. They could easily break the trail but he wasn't sure if they'd be able to break all of them before one was detonated. They ran a huge risk of being caught in an explosion if they tried. The more he looked around the more trails he saw, all leading toward the volcano, all with many repeaters. JJ knew they could repair the portal quickly and decided it was the best plan. The quicker they could get out of the Minecraft world the better. "Let's hurry," he called to the others.

Max moved close to the portal. She opened her inventory and started placing the obsidian blocks.

In no time the frame was five blocks high and she added in the final blocks to the top of the frame.

She removed the flint and steel from her inventory and in an instant a whoosh went up and the portal flickered and crackled to life.

Max turned to face the Crafters' Club members.

"Thank you so much," she said. "It has been fantastic to meet you and share an adventure."

Jamie laughed. "It might not be over yet. Who knows where this portal will take you."

Max smiled. "Hopefully back to Felix so I can tell him to stop blowing up the map."

"But," Annie asked, "how will we know if you get home safely?"

"I know," Charli said. "Come back into the map on Xbox Live and leave us a message. Create a sign or something and let us know if you are home and if Felix is with you."

"Great idea," Jamie said. "That way if we don't hear from you we can come back in and search the maps. Try to help you."

"You are very good friends," Max said. "One day I hope I can introduce you to Felix."

"JJ?" Jamie's voice was harsh. "You're being rude, aren't you going to say goodbye to Max?"

JJ glanced back to the group. "Sorry." He pointed in the direction of the redstone dust. "That's just got me really worried. We need to break sections of it."

The group turned to look where JJ pointed.

"It's Felix's last resort," Max said. "It all leads to the volcano and will cause an enormous explosion if he detonates it. There will be a warning though. He said he will set off five smaller explosions first to warn that the huge one is coming."

"That's a relief," JJ said. "I was worried it could go off any second. It's time for you to go, Max. We need to build a new portal that hopefully will take us back to our home."

Max's reply was lost by the sound of an explosion. It was on the other side of the village. The ground was still shaking when the second explosion sounded, then the third, fourth, and fifth.

"Oh no," Max cried. "It's the signal. Felix is going to destroy the map."

There was no time to make a plan.

"Run, Max!" Jamie yelled. He pushed her in the direction of the portal. The black-and-white panda sprinted into the purple glow and disappeared.

The Crafters' Club members stood still. There was nothing they could do. An eerie silence came over the map momentarily before it was rocked by an explosion so huge JJ felt his teeth rattle. His vision blurred and his breath was taken from him as he was flung backward, twisting through the air.

Jamie's stomach twisted in knots as the explosion flung and spun him. It was over. Finally, after all the wonderful adventures they'd had, their time in the Minecraft world had come to an end. It was so disappointing. He waited, expecting at any moment to stop spinning and to arrive in the clearing near his and JJ's house.

A final spin and he felt himself crash to the ground. His eyes were closed. He didn't want to open them. Didn't want it to be the end of the best thing that had ever happened to him.

"Jamie."

"Jamie!"

He heard Annie then Charli call out his name. He knew they'd be as upset as he was.

"Come on," JJ's voice broke into his thoughts.

"We're weak and we need your help."

"Weak?" What did he mean? He forced his eyes open. Instead of being greeted by the thick trees of the forest behind his house he was surrounded by the blocky Minecraft world. Charli was already busy building a portal.

He pulled himself up to his feet. "We didn't die?"

JJ grinned. "Nope. We ended up in another map. Another glitch I guess. This adventure has been full of them. At least this was a good one, but we're not hanging around. Once the portal's ready we're going home."

The two brothers moved across and helped Charli and Annie place the final blocks for the portal. They lit it and without any discussion stepped straight into its welcoming glow.

CHAPTER SIX

Real World

"Phew," Annie said as they tumbled onto the soft grass beside the clearing. "Thank goodness we made it back."

"And we didn't die," Jamie said. "I wonder if the portal took Max home?" His eyes scoured the clearing. "Definitely no sign of her here."

"What happened?" Annie asked. "Why didn't we die? We should have, shouldn't we?"

JJ shrugged. "Our adventure was full of glitches. It was great in one way as it meant that we didn't die, but scary in another. Who knows what might happen another time. We'll have to think very carefully before going back in."

"Fingers crossed Max is back home with her family and Felix," Charli said. "I wonder what it's like in the Philippines? We should use Google Earth and check it out." She laughed. "It would kind of be like flying around."

"No." Jamie said. "What a waste of time. If Max can travel here through a portal then we should go and visit her. I'd love to see a different country. I wonder what they eat?"

"Speaking of food, I'm starving." Annie rubbed her stomach and turned to JJ. "Did your dad really say he was baking a cake?"

JJ nodded. "Sure did. Let's go back and see if it's ready."

Ten minutes later the four Crafters' Club members sat in the family room. Annie's eyes nearly bulged out of her head when JJ's dad brought in a tray containing the largest chocolate–raspberry layered cake she'd ever seen. That, plus four choc-berry milkshakes, and it was a meal to drool over.

The television screen showed the map Felix's explosions had been destroying. It didn't look like much of the volcano or its surrounds still existed.

"I think you should move over to the portal Max went through," Jamie said. "If she comes back in it will be through that portal."

"Good idea." JJ moved JJLee45 over by the portal.

They munched their cake and slurped their milkshakes as they waited.

"Do you think we're allowed seconds?" Annie asked, eyeing the remains of the cake. "This is too good to eat only one slice."

JJ laughed. "The fact my dad left it in here means he's either crazy or he expects us to eat more. Help yourself."

Annie cut herself another large slice. She let out a contented sigh as she melted back into the couch and lifted the delicious cake to her lips.

"Look," Charli said.

They all turned their attention to the screen. Pandy11 had just come through the portal.

"I hope that's her playing from the Xbox and not the real Max," JJ said.

They continued to watch. Pandy11 opened her inventory and took out a sign. She placed it on the ground next to JJLee45: Home safely, Felix here too.

The Crafters' Club members all cheered.

Max placed another sign: He's sorry he blew us up, he thought he was saving me. He couldn't see us. Glitching?

"You'd better write something back," Charli said.

JJ was already creating a sign. It read: So happy everyone is home and not hurt. It was an awesome adventure.

Pandy11 jumped up and down on the spot causing the four friends to laugh.

"I think she's agreeing that it was awesome," Annie said. "I wonder if we'll ever see her again."

"Definitely," Jamie said. "We should organize something now. Write another sign, JJ. Suggest we meet in the map tomorrow."

JJ stared at his brother. "Are you sure that's a good idea? We fixed things this time but we might not be so lucky next time. We might end up in the Philippines or Max and Felix might end up stuck here. I'm worried that the glitches are occurring because we're on Xbox Live and that's the only way we can meet up with Max and Felix."

Jamie shook his head. "Don't be silly, we always work out a solution in the end."

"He's right," Charli said. "We've had lots of near misses, but no disasters."

"Yet," JJ said.

"Anyway, it's too late," Annie said. "Look, she's going."

The four turned their attention back to the screen. Max had put up one last sign and now looked like she was waving as she stepped back into the portal.

"Love that I have new friends," Annie read the sign. "Let's join up on Xbox Live again and plan another adventure. I want to introduce you all to Felix."

Jamie grinned. "See, Max is just like me. She loves adventures. I hope Felix is as much fun."

"I guess we're going to find out." Annie finished the last few crumbs on her plate then turned her attention back to the remains of the gooey layered cake. "That cake really is sensational and your dad still hasn't come to collect it. Do you think–"

She didn't get to finish her sentence. She was met with a battering of cushions and three very convincing shouts of "No!"

Other Books by Louise Guy

The Crafters' Club Series

Two Worlds, The Villagers, Lost
The Professor, Spirit, Friendship
The Secret, The Promise, The End
Worlds Collide

The Secret World of Curly Jones

New Worlds
Old Worlds

Louise Also Writes for Adults!

Everyday Lies
Fortunate Friends

For more information and to purchase books, visit:

www.LouiseGuy.com.

Acknowledgments

Thank you to Ray, JJ and Jamie for their knowledge, interest and enthusiasm for all things Minecraft.

A very special thank you to the **awesome** Finn and Rocky for their feedback on early drafts of the story.

Sincere thanks to Kat Betts of Element Editing Services for your editing and suggestions for improvement of this story.

And most importantly, thank you to all of the readers who have requested the continuation of the Crafters' Club series. You are the reason that this special edition has been produced.

Made in the USA
San Bernardino, CA
16 August 2018